Tree of Cranes

WRITTEN AND ILLUSTRATED BY

ALLEN SAY

SCHOLASTIC BOOK CLUB EDITION

ISBN 0-590-46237-7

12 11 10 9 8 7 6 5 4 3 2 1   2 3 4 5 6 7/9

Printed in the U.S.A.   36

First Scholastic printing, November 1992

To Master Noro Shinpei

When I was not yet old enough to wear long pants, Mama always worried that I might drown in a neighbor's pond. Time and again she warned me not to play there, but I never listened because the pond was filled with carp of bright colors.

The last time I went there was a gray winter day, too cold for the fish to move around. They never came out from under the rocks, and all I caught was a bad chill.

Mama would be upset with me, I knew. She
would know right away how I got my mittens all wet.
But then she might be happy just to see me.
"Mama, I'm home!" I called. There was no answer.
She always met me at the porch, always. I
called again, and finally she answered, sounding far
away. I waited, but she didn't come out to see me.
She must be sick, I thought.

Mama was in the living room, folding origami paper. She just nodded, barely looking at me. But there were two slices of my favorite tea cake waiting for me. That made me feel better.

"Why are you making cranes?" I asked.

"Because I want to make a big wish," she said without looking up.

"You're going to fold a thousand cranes to make your wish come true?"

"Maybe even two thousand . . ." She reached out and touched my face with her cool hand.

"Why, you're hot all over." Mama frowned and gave me a silent stare.

I hung my head and said nothing. She knew.

Anytime Mama thought I had a cold it was time
for a hot bath.

"Ten whole minutes and not one second less,"
she told me.

She was upset. She didn't even rinse my back.
Her slippers went shuffling all the way down
the hallway. Then a door closed shut. She wasn't
coming back to keep me company.

I'd better say I'm sorry, I thought to myself.

But before I could apologize, Mama put me in my nightclothes!

"I don't want to go to bed!"

"You need to stay nice and warm."

"All afternoon?"

"All afternoon."

"Will you read me stories?"

"No stories. But I'll make you hot lunch."

I knew what that meant. Rice gruel. Only sick people ate rice gruel.

And that's what I had, with a sour plum and yellow radishes, eating all alone and drinking hot tea in Papa's big cup.

Then I lay down facing the door and hoped and hoped Mama would come back with an apple and peel the skin in a long strip like a red ribbon and then read me a story.

The door never opened.

"Mama!" I called finally. She didn't answer.

After a long while I heard a noise coming from the garden. Maybe the old gardener had come to clip our trees again. I got up and opened the window.

It was snowing outside. And Mama was digging around a small tree.

"What are you doing?" I shouted.

Mama stopped and stared.

"Close that window this second and go straight back to bed!"

Quickly I closed the window and lay down again. She's really angry now, I thought. But why is she gardening in the snow? Is she digging a hole because she's angry with me? I didn't know what to think.

I was nearly asleep when Mama came in. She was
carrying a tree in a blue pot. It was the little pine
Mama and Papa had planted when I was born, so I would
live a long life like the tree.

"What are you doing with my tree?" I asked.

"You'll see," she said, setting down the pot.
"Do you know what today is?"

"Ah . . . seven days before the New Year's Day."

"That's right," she said, and smiled! Then she
fetched the silver cranes and some sewing things from
the living room.

Finally Mama sat down. She put a thread through
one of the cranes and hung it from the tree.
    "I have been acting strangely all day,"
she said. I started to reply, but she shushed me.
"If you promise to stay in bed, I will tell you why."
    "I promise," I said.
    "I was born and lived far away in another country,
long before I came here and met your father."
    "Where?"
    "A warm place called Ca-li-for-ni-a," she whispered.
    I nodded.
    "Today is a very special day in that warm place.
If you happened to be there now, you would see trees like
this everywhere, all decorated with winking lights
and small globes of silver and gold . . .

"And under each tree there are boxes of presents people give to friends and loved ones."

"I want a samurai kite!" I said.

"You give and receive, child. It is a day of love and peace. Strangers smile at one another. Enemies stop fighting. We need more days like it." She put the last crane on the tree.

"It's wonderful!" I cried.

"It's not finished," she said. And she brought some candles from the kitchen and tied them to the branches.

"Are you going to burn my tree?" I asked.

Mama laughed. "Just the candles, and only for a short while. We'll replant your tree tomorrow."

"I want to light them! May I, may I?"

"Do it quickly then."

Mama let me strike the matches. And when all the candles were lit, she fell silent. She was remembering. She was seeing another tree in a faraway place where she had been small like me.

Mama held me in her lap. The cranes turned slowly, flashing candlelight. There couldn't be a tree more beautiful than mine, I thought. Not even in the place where Mama was born.

"What present would you like?" I asked.

"Only peace and quiet," Mama said.

"I mean something from me."

"Oh, something very, very special . . . like a promise."

"I said I would stay in bed."

"Another promise, then."

"All right."

"Give me your word you'll never go to the pond again."

I promised.

I was fast asleep when Papa came home.

Next morning I jumped out of bed because a
fierce warrior was staring at me. But it was only
a kite.

Only a kite! The one I'd always wanted! Then
I saw the tree behind it, my tree. Suddenly I
remembered last night and all that Mama had told me.

Thank you, Mama! Thank you, Papa!

I ran outside with my present.

Outside, everything was covered with snow.

"There'll be another day," Mama said. "A fine windy day with no snow."

"Plenty of snow to make a snowman!" Papa said. "Let's make one together."

And like the snowman we made, many years have
melted away now. But I will always remember
that day of peace and quiet. It was my first Christmas.